T0380510

Succeeding Against All Odds

DANIELLE VERRET

Copyright © 2020 by Danielle Verret. 807759

All rights reserved. No part of this book may
be reproduced or transmitted in any form or by
any means, electronic or mechanical, including
photocopying, recording, or by any information storage
and retrieval system, without permission in writing from
the copyright owner.

This is a work of fiction. Names, characters,
places and incidents either are the product of the
author's imagination or are used fictitiously, and any
resemblance to any actual persons, living or dead,
events, or locales is entirely coincidental.

To order additional copies of this book, contact:
Xlibris
1-888-795-4274
www.Xlibris.com
Orders@Xlibris.com

ISBN: Softcover   978-1-7960-8237-1
       EBook   978-1-7960-8236-4

Print information available on the last page

Rev. date: 01/24/2020

Succeeding against all odds

By Danielle Verret

On a beautiful island, named CarlaRossa, not far away from United States soil; a young lady named Sophia sprung forth into existence. Born from humble parents, both her Mom and Dad were teachers; her family strove to make ends meet, as their two young daughters were coming of age.

Sophia, being the second daughter, was an able, energetic, determined child who wanted to succeed; at whatever task, that she would find herself undertaking. She learned to cook at an early age, having been taught by the maidservants that worked in the family's home.

She did somewhat well in school, but not to the point of academic excellence. Overall she worked hard to make the grade, as she got along fine with her peers.

As Sophia grew up, when she turned nine years old, the situation at her abode had taken a dramatic turn. Her father had now left the house, to live overseas on a government contract, in the hope of being able to provide stronger financial support for the family. Her mother, on the other hand, was left alone; to take care of their two young daughters.

Things went smooth, within the first year of her father's absence, but when Sophia's father returned the following year; she became really concerned, because she had found out that her mother was pregnant with another child.

As years went by, Sophia developed into a teenager. She then went on to become very jealous and envious, of her baby sister. The reason being as such, is that their father, Robert, began sending more allowance money; to his younger last born daughter, Belinda, while neglecting Sophia's adolescent wants and needs. Sophia, now flourishing intd young womanhood, started going down the path into rebellion. She started going out with older men, sleeping with them on occasion for gifts or money, without tying the knot.

The time period, that these events were occurring, was in the 1950's; and during that epoch, young women were subjected to intense scrutiny by society, when they engaged in such sexual acts, and especially if they inhabited, lesser developing countries.

Sophia, eventually married a man, who showed some interest in her, in order to save face, and to bring back honor to her family's name. Soon after, she went on to migrate to the West Coast, on the mainland of the United States.

As the couple entered the mainland; Sophia and her new husband, Joshua, quickly settled in the outskirts of the city, in a suburb, named Happytown, on the West Coast. Joshua began working at a variety of odd jobs; to maintain and sustain his wife. Within two years of their marriage, Sophia bore a child, whom she dearly named Elaina. Her husband, Joshua, adored his little girl, Elaina. He was very attentive and caring towards her. She was daddy's baby girl, always tending to her every wants and needs.

The next five years of Elaina's life were full of affection and tender love, demonstrated mainly by her father. Her mother, Sophia, on the other hand, was not quite content. Her husband, Joshua, held a variety of jobs; but never managed to secure any prestigious position. Sophia, on her side, did find work; these jobs, however, were menial; and most definitely would not and could not, help her to achieve the lifestyle that she wanted to pursue.

She had wished to purchase her own home, dress luxuriously and to hold weekend get-togethers and parties at home, her husband, Joshua, though would not adhere to that.

As a result, Sophia in her realm of friends and acquaintances, looked for another man; and indeed found one. She met a man, by the name of Martin, whom she thought was pleasant and very admirable. She started dating Martin, on a weekly basis, while her husband left for work.

Martin, first appeared in the house to Joshua, as someone Sophia's family had known in their old country. He looked like a refined, polished and courteous man in his mid-thirties. He exhibited a caring attitude, towards daughter Elaina; always bringing presents to her, as if to please mother Sophia.

With time passing, Sophia's feelings began to succumb to this handsome built man, who had happened to be an import-export executive. Within a year of their courtship: Sophia decided to leave her husband. Joshua, to go on living with Martin. She abandoned the apartment, where she was living with Joshua; and along with daughter Elaina; she left to settle across town with her new boyfriend Martin.

The two went on to live in a beautifully renovated hi-rise building, not too far from the coastal beach. After two years of togetherness, Martin and Sophia conceived a child; and this child being born out of wedlock was named Amanda.

When Amanda was born, father Martin was now beginning to switch his attention from Elaina; which was Sophia's first daughter with Joshua, to his own daughter Amanda. Martin, consequently, was not just not paying attention to Elaina, and all her needs, at this time; but was actually mistreating her, yelling, screaming and hitting her at every mistake or mishap the child was committing.

At first, Sophia did not really take notice of Martin's mistreatment of Elaina. First and foremost, she was consumed, taking care of their new daughter Amanda. Sophia mostly cared about the times that she and Martin spent together, having fun; going out to parties; having parties at home; to the point, where Martin was often drunk and unable to go back to work the next day.

Sophia also loved having beautiful furniture, acquiring china, possessing lavish clothing that Martin was able to purchase for her. Sophia, at this period in her life, enjoyed being a housewife; cleaning and cooking delicious and tasty dishes; for her boyfriend, lover and husband-to-be. Martin, however, was a married man; separated from his wife, but living with Sophia as his mistress.

One day, he broke his silence, by telling Sophia that he would not divorce his wife to marry her. A few months later, Sophia became totally disillusioned with her live-in relationship; and she was looking for a way out of Martin's life; along with her two children, Elaina and Amanda.

Martin soon heard and felt that Sophia might have second thoughts about their living together; having a child out of wedlock, and not wanting to marry her, not even for the sake of their daughter Amanda.

He now began to change his attitude completely towards her. He started yelling at Sophia, cursing and hitting her in the living room, in the bedroom, in the presence of the two children, threatening them and even hitting his own child, Amanda. While drinking on occasion, Martin hit Sophia on the head, at times. Sophia being afraid, did not retaliate, she did not go to the hospital to report him; instead she treated herself by applying some over-the-counter medicines and other home remedies that she knew of.

Sophia was very devoted to Martin, but she learned to leave him. She came to the realization that he would not cooperate in changing his behavior; for the better; as she reckoned to reason with him, time and time again. Ultimately, Sophia decided to make a transition; from devoting her life to an uncaring, abusive, destructive, lover relationship, to a woman free of co-dependency.

She left Martin, one day, packing all her belongings, along with her two children. She had a friend wait for her, outside of their apartment, after Martin had left for work. The friend had brought a big van with him; and Sophia was able to pack all her stuff in that van; leaving the apartment, without posting any kind of notice to Martin.

She then went on, to drop most of her belongings; into a relative's house, then checked into a shelter; along with her two daughters.

Shelter life was not easy to adapt to, especially with two children, under Sophia's care. But mother Sophia had learned to pray to God for guidance. She was rescued, one day, by two church elders; who were preaching in the cafeteria, where she was eating with her children. They offered to aid and assist her, throughout this difficult period of her life.

With their utmost devotion, Sophia was eventually baptized at a local congregation, whereby she felt so elated, that she cried in triumph. She intensely felt God's presence, Jesus Christ and the Holy Spirit; guiding her incessantly, through her every move, at this particular time in her life.

After her baptism, Sophia was able to obtain her own apartment; with the help of the church, for her comfort and the well-being of her children. Sophia was now on her way to becoming self-reliant, while also gaining complete freedom from a terrifying past relationship with her former lover, Martin.

She did not press charges against Martin, for hitting her in the head. She did suffer, however, from pains and aches in the head from time to time. One day, her head pain was so intense; she rushed to the hospital's emergency room for treatment, where immediately she was admitted. The doctors discovered a tumor lodging in the back of her head, which required an immediate operation.

Sophia underwent the operation, quite successfully. The tumor was removed; and she was able to come out of the hospital, within a couple of days. Sophia took three months, however, to fully recover after the tumor was removed.

Thereafter, she was able to perform many of her daily routine activities.

Her greatest triumph was achieved when she came to the realization that her friendship with God and Jesus Christ, his Son, was priceless. She also gained real inner peace and joy from knowing them. She also experienced much happiness from associating with other true worshippers of God and Jesus Christ in the church.

Soon after, her recovery from the head operation, she was able to matriculate into a course of study; at a four year college, located within her vicinity. Her chosen field was to pursue a Domestic violence prevention counselor (social work) program that would lead her to a degree. She was on her way, to a course of action; that would take her to total independence and complete success in the future. During her four years of studies, she received tremendous support in bringing up her two daughters. Her fellow church members, always gave her a helping hand with the children. Some watched Amanda, while Mommy Sophia was studying or preparing for exams; others assisted daughter Elaina, by helping her to complete her most difficult math homework.

Sophia eventually graduated from college, and was able to pass her state certification; with flying colors. Thereafter, she managed to procure a high paying position; with a national government agency, located in the neighboring town.

Sophia was truly blessed, as she overcame all the obstacles that had come upon her. In the end, she wholeheartedly gave praise to the God of Abraham, Isaac and Jacob for her ultimate success.

As she mentioned to her children; and to the congregation at large; once and for all, as she was giving her testimony, she declared; "I can confirm that God has blessed me as a single parent. He really does come to the rescue of the afflicted and the fatherless". "I thank him overwhelmingly".

And as her daughter, Elaina, the oldest of the two, stood by watching her Mom speak to the congregation; with such courage and dignity, she uttered her own gratitude to the Almighty by saying; "God you are with us, so everything will always be all right".

Printed in the United States
By Bookmasters